DINOSAUR CLUB

The Compsognathus Chase

Written by Rex Stone
Illustrated by Louise Forshaw

Jamie has just moved to Ammonite Bay, a
stretch of coastline famed for its fossils. Jamie is
a member of Dinosaur Club—a network of
kids who share dinosaur knowledge, help identify
fossils, post new discoveries, and chat about
all things prehistoric. Jamie carries his tablet
everywhere in case he needs to contact the club.

Jamie is exploring Ammonite Bay when he
meets Tess, another member of Dinosaur Club.
Tess takes Jamie to a cave with a strange tunnel
and some dinosaur footprints. When they walk
along the footprints, the two new friends find
themselves back in the time of the dinosaurs!

It's amazing, but dangerous too—and they'll
definitely need help from Dinosaur Club…

CONTENTS

CHAPTER 1

The Dinosaur Museum was alive with
dinosaurs—tiny T. rex, a small pack of
diplodocuses, grounded miniature
pterosaurs, and a velociraptor arguing
with a stegosaurus over who had the
better costume. Jamie Morgan and his
best friend Tess Clay were herding them
all into the activity room.

"I've never seen so many people here," exclaimed Jamie.

Tess laughed as a little triceratops with lopsided horns raced by. "Dress as a Dino Day was a great idea of your mom's."

The two friends squeezed in at the back of the room as the children watched Jamie's mom show film clips about the Jurassic period. Computer-generated stegosaurs lumbered across the screen, then a pack of allosaurs attacked a huge diplodocus.

"Now," said Dr. Morgan. "Let's look at the landscape. It's just as exciting." The film showed a picture of a huge land mass. "This is Pangaea," she told her wide-eyed audience. "There were no separate continents in the world like there are today—just this lump of land. But that was about to change."

BOOM!

An erupting volcano appeared on the screen. Shrieks of delight filled the room.

"The volcanoes and earthquakes broke up Pangaea like a jigsaw puzzle," said Dr. Morgan. "That was the start of the continents we know today. And now it's time for lunch!" she announced. "There are sandwiches and chips at the back, so if you get into a line…"

But the young dinosaurs weren't listening. They jumped out of their seats and surged toward the food, chattering excitedly.

"Here we go" muttered Tess.

Jamie and Tess leaped into action. It was their job to make sure every child had a napkin, a plate, and a sandwich. But a sea of hands was trying to snatch the food all at once.

"Slow down," Jamie shouted above the din.

"ROARRR," answered an ankylosaurus who leaped up to grab an extra pack of chips from the box in Tess's hand.

"Dinosaurs fight to get their food," growled a stegosaurus, pushing to the front.

"That's not always true," said Jamie, giving Tess a grin.

The children stopped and stared at him.
"Real dinosaurs, like ankylosaurus,
make a nice straight line and march one
behind the other," Jamie told them
solemnly. "I should know. I live upstairs,
above the Dinosaur Museum."

The dinosaurs immediately shuffled into a line, arms—and wings—by their sides.

"That was brilliant!" Tess whispered to Jamie as he poured juice into velociraptor-patterned cups. "I thought we were going to be trampled."

Soon all the children had marched off, with some very realistic roaring, to eat their lunch.

Jamie stared at the image that was still on the screen—the huge mountain ranges of the Jurassic period that were formed by continents crashing into each other.

"No wonder the kids got excited," he said, taking a handful of chips. "Mom's presentation was awesome."

"Should we check out some real Jurassic mountains?" Tess whispered.

"Good idea," Jamie agreed. 'We haven't explored the mountains in Dino World yet.'

The two friends had a secret. Deep in the cliffs of Dinosaur Cove, they had found the entrance to a magical world of living dinosaurs. The only other people who knew about it were their friends in Dinosaur Club, a network of dinosaur fans from around the world.

Jamie grinned. "We've helped with lunch like we promised..."

At that moment, Dr. Morgan rushed past. "I forgot to tell them to wash their hands before they hit the museum!"

"We're just going out for a bit," Jamie told her.

"Okay, see you later!" And with that, Dr. Morgan was gone.

Tess held up her Jurassic ammonite, which would take them into the right dino time. Jamie checked to make sure his tablet and his notebook were in his backpack. "Ready!" he said.

Tess snatched up some tuna sandwiches. "We'll need lunch too," she said, tucking them into the backpack.

Outside, the two friends scrambled up the dry streambed that led to the secret smugglers' cave, and then began to climb the boulders. Jamie reached for a handhold to pull himself over a ledge.

CRACK!

The rock split off in his hand and he lost his grip. Jamie was dangling by only one arm, high above the ground!

CHAPTER 2

Tess shot out a hand and grabbed Jamie's arm with a firm grip.

"Thanks!" breathed Jamie, scrambling for safety as loose rock and pebbles rattled away down the boulders. "One rock cracks and I nearly fall down the cliff. Imagine what it must have been like when all of Pangaea split apart and bits of it collided!"

Climbing more carefully now, they pulled themselves up to the smugglers' cave and into the secret chamber.

"There are Wanna's footprints, waiting for us," said Jamie, placing his sneakers over the shallow dips on the rocky floor. He felt the usual bubble of excitement as they followed the line of prints to the cave wall and…

A blast of hot air hit their faces and they found themselves stepping out of Ginkgo Cave among the giant trees of the Jurassic.

"Wow!" panted Tess, wiping her forehead. "It's steamier than ever."

"The trees are dripping with water," said Jamie. "Looks like we just missed a rainstorm."

Flickers of sunlight were breaking through the leaves of the huge trees above, and drops of water plopped down on their heads. Suddenly they heard a rustling sound from the ferns in front of them. Spray flew up and soaked them as a dripping wet, green and brown dinosaur charged out of the undergrowth and skidded to a halt at their feet.

"Wanna!" exclaimed Jamie, wiping his face. "Thanks for the shower."

"Want to come mountaineering with us?" Tess asked, giving their dinosaur friend a scratch on his flat, bony head.

Grunk!

"I think that's a yes!" Jamie laughed as Wanna ran around in excited circles.

"The Misty Mountains are
to the north." Tess checked her
compass. "This way."

They soon reached the edge of
the stifling jungle. Ahead, the flat plains
steamed in the heat, and beyond rose the
high peaks of the conelike mountains,
purple against the sky.

"They're awesome," said Jamie. "And
look at those dark clouds above them. I
bet there's another storm coming."

"I think the dinosaurs have sensed it,"
agreed Tess, peering intently through her
binoculars. "There's hardly anything
stirring on the plains today."

"What are we waiting for?" asked
Jamie. "We don't want to get caught in
the open by a prehistoric downpour."

They set off sprinting across the plains, splashing through the puddles made by the rain. Wanna galloped ahead. At last they reached the green lower slopes of the Misty Mountains.

Jamie gazed up at the rugged peaks towering above them, disappearing into the clouds. "What a sight!" he breathed.

Grunk! The little dinosaur stopped and looked up as if puzzled.

"Yes, that's where we're heading, Wanna," said Tess.

They started climbing through thick ferns, disturbing huge, brightly colored insects as they went. But Wanna hung back.

"Come on," Jamie called to him. "It's just getting a bit steep. You'll be okay."

The little dinosaur hesitated for a moment, then he trotted along behind them, staying close on their heels.

Soon, the vegetation stopped, and they were clambering up the bare rocks alongside a pebbly stream. Wanna poked his head in and gulped noisily.

Jamie stopped and looked back to where the Great Canyon ran across the plains down to the ocean. "The stream's flowing down to the canyon," he said.

"Today history is being made," announced Tess, speaking into an imaginary microphone. "Our intrepid Jurassic trio are exploring the Misty Mountains. They are the only humans— and wannanosaurus—ever to attempt such a climb. Steam is rising from the mountainside as rainwater evaporates. What will they find? Does anything live in this strange place?"

EEK, EEK!

A shrill squawk filled the air. All three
of them froze.

CHAPTER 3

A beaky brown nose poked out from the steaming ferns. Then, a whole head appeared, with little bright eyes that swiveled this way and that, checking the area. Finally a strange creature, no bigger than a turkey, stalked out and shook itself. It took no notice of the two friends or Wanna, but scuttled away on stiff back legs toward the pebbly stream. Jamie and

Tess snorted with laughter as its head
darted down to drink, and its tail bobbed
up in the air.

Wanna cocked his head to one side.
He looked puzzled.

"Have you ever seen anything so funny?" asked Jamie, laughing.

"It walks like a cartoon dinosaur!" Tess spluttered. "What is it?"

Jamie took his tablet out of his backpack and snapped a picture. He opened the Dinosaur Club app and sent the photo to their friends.

"Anyone know what this dino could be?"

Olek from Poland replied with the name of the dinosaur:

"Compsognathus."

"It means pretty jaw" wrote Chloe from Australia.

"I wouldn't call that pretty!" Tess scoffed.

"It's really fast," Chinelo from Nigeria wrote, "even though it's one of the smallest dinos. And it's a carnivore."

Jamie typed another message to thank them. As he stuffed his tablet into his backpack, another beaky head popped out of the ferns.

"Looks like it's got a friend," said Tess. The newcomer scuttled over to the water, squawking. "I wonder what they'll do if we go up to them."

She began to climb over a rock to get to the drinking dinosaurs. But her foot slipped on some loose stones.

"Yaieee!" she yelped as she stumbled. Immediately, the two heads shot up and two pairs of beady eyes studied Tess.

Yaieee! Yaieee! the creatures
called back.

"Wow!" Jamie said as he hauled Tess
to her feet. "They're copying you."

Tess made the noise again. This time
four more heads appeared and all the
compsognathus joined in with the
sound. Soon the calls of the mimicking
dinos were bouncing off the rocks.

"You know how experts think some
dinosaurs evolved into birds," said Tess,
admiringly. "I bet these compsos
became parrots!"

Wanna darted after a green-and-yellow striped lizard that scurried away from the stream, grunking excitedly.

"That lizard has a purple head!" exclaimed Tess. "I've never seen anything like that before."

EEK, EEK!

The compsognathus had seen it too. They scampered toward it in a bunch, shrieking as the lizard zigzagged over rocks and under ferns, trying to escape.

"That lizard better watch out," said Jamie, "or he's going to be compso lunch!" Wanna was left behind as the eager little dinos raced along after it.

"And the compsognathus are gaining on their prey," announced Tess into her pretend microphone. "More have appeared. They're fighting over it... can you hear that angry chattering? I think it's going to get away... No, the smallest compso has caught the lizard and now he has all the others after him."

The little compsognathus dashed past them, lizard tail dangling from its mouth, pursued by the others.

Jamie laughed. "They remind me of the kids at the museum—obsessed with food."

"And you told them that dinosaurs get in an orderly line," said Tess. "I'm glad they can't see what really happens."

The compsognathus gulped the lizard down and the chase ended. The rest of the bunch began sniffing around, looking for more food. Then one strutted eagerly toward Jamie and Tess.

"Look out," said Jamie. "We've got company."

"It looks like a mini ostrich," said Tess, as the little dino stalked around them, neck outstretched, sniffing their scent.

"It's very friendly," said Jamie. "And quite cute… Aah!" He leaped in alarm as the dinosaur suddenly jumped onto his back with a screech. "Help!" he yelled. "Its claws are really digging in."

The determined compsognathus started scratching at the top of Jamie's backpack.

"It's going after the sandwiches," called Tess. "Oh no you don't, you little thief." She grabbed the birdlike dinosaur by its waist and tugged. But it was surprisingly strong, and clung on with its long claws. Jamie's arms flailed around as he tried to knock the dino off, and Wanna grunked anxiously around their feet.

At last, Tess tugged really hard, pulling
the backpack right off Jamie's back. The
compsognathus let go as the backpack
crashed to the ground. Tess grabbed the
pack as the determined dinosaur looked
the friends up and down, searching for a
way to get its snack.

Wanna grunked crossly at it, then waddled away up the steep mountainside.

"Good thinking, Wanna," said Tess, putting the backpack onto her shoulders as Jamie rubbed at the scratches the little dino had left. "Let's go before any more get the idea that we're a sandwich shop."

"Agreed," said Jamie grimly. "Those compsos are not as cute as I thought."

They set off after Wanna but soon heard shrieks all around. They found themselves surrounded by a whole crowd of chattering dinosaurs.

Compsognathus darted out of the ferns
and leaped at them from every rock
and stone.

"Uh oh" whispered Jamie. "We're in
big trouble now."

CHAPTER 4

EEK, EEK!

The little creatures jostled against Tess and Jamie, pecking and scratching at their legs.

"We can't make a run for it," said Tess, looking around at the carpet of chirping dinosaurs. "There's nowhere to put our feet."

"They are just like the pesky kids at the museum," said Jamie. "And that's given me an idea." He reached into the backpack on Tess's shoulders, pulled out a tuna sandwich and waved it at the dinos. When he had their attention, he tossed it into the ferns. The compsognathus chased it like a swarm of bees.

"Well done," said Tess. "Let's get away from here while they're busy fighting for it."

"Too late," groaned Jamie. "They're coming back for more. Ouch!"

The hungry little compsognathuses were back, raking their sharp claws against Jamie and Tess's knees.

"They don't mean any harm," said Tess, trying to push them away, "but that hurts."

Grunk, GRUNK!

Wanna was back, running around the crowd, trying to get to the friends.

"Ow!" Tess was suddenly pulled sideways. "What's going on?"

"One of them has got the backpack strap," called Jamie. "They want more sandwiches."

The hungry dinosaur gave a tug. Tess staggered as she tried to wrench the strap away. But now compsognathus from all around were joining in the tug-of-war, and Tess was no match for them.

"Help!" Tess cried as she lost her balance and crashed to the ground. Soon she was covered in chirping dinosaurs all searching for food.

Grunk! Wanna came to her rescue. He butted and pushed the little dinos away. Jamie saw his chance. He grabbed Tess's arm and pulled her to her feet.

"Thanks…both of you…" Tess was out of breath.

"How are we going to escape?" Jamie wondered. "They're everywhere."

"Let's try the tuna decoy again," said Tess, taking Jamie's backpack off and reaching into it. "I'll try to throw the sandwich a bit farther this time." She lobbed it deep into the nearby ferns.

Some of the compsognathus scampered off and started hunting for it.

"Run!" shouted Jamie, grabbing his backpack. "While we've got the chance."

But the other compsognathus weren't so easily fooled. They chased after the friends.

"Let's jump in the stream!" yelled Tess. "Maybe they don't like getting wet."

They splashed into the shallow water
that trickled down from the mountain.

"It's working!" said Jamie, looking
over his shoulder. "They've stopped."

The compsognathus were leaping
around on the bank, squeaking and
chattering crossly, but they didn't follow.

Tess, Jamie, and Wanna splashed
upstream. Soon, they had left the
annoying little dinos behind. The banks
were becoming higher as they climbed.

"Hey! Have you noticed something strange?" asked Tess. "The water's warm— really warm."

"You're right," agreed Jamie. "Even though it's ice melted from the top of the mountain." He peered up the streambed. "It's much steeper now."

"And rockier." Tess looked down at the jagged stones beneath their feet. "See the way the rocks look different? It sort of looks like lots of lumps of rock are fused together."

"I remember Mom telling us about that," agreed Jamie. "It sounds like it's solidified volcanic ash."

They looked at each other.

"That means…" began Jamie.

"Misty Mountain isn't just a mountain…" said Tess.

"It's a dormant volcano," finished Jamie. "Awesome!"

"I'd love to have seen it erupt," said Tess, her eyes shining. "There would have been rumbling and shaking and rivers of lava streaming down."

"Let's see if we can make it to the crater at the top," said Jamie.

They scrambled over boulders, sneakers slipping on the wet ground. Wanna kept close behind.

"Wow!" gasped Jamie. "Can you smell that?"

Tess flapped her hand in front of her face. "It's like rotten eggs," she said. "It smells even worse than ginkgo."

"What is it?" Jamie was holding his nose now.

GRUNK!

Wanna stopped. He was trembling with fright, his eyes wild.

GRUNK, GRUNK!

"What's the matter, Wanna?" asked
Jamie. "Something's really bothering
him." Wanna dashed down the volcano
and the friends hurried after him, worried.

Then, the ground beneath them
began to shake.

RUMMMMMBLE!

"It feels like an earthquake!" cried
Jamie, staggering on the shuddering rock.
"Wanna must have sensed it before
we did."

"Help!" Jamie and Tess went
sprawling on the rocks. Wanna only kept
his balance by spreading all four paws
out wide.

The shaking stopped as suddenly as it had started.

Jamie jumped to his feet. "Wait!" he exclaimed. "Hot ground, steamy rainwater, thick mist, strangely quiet plains." Tess looked over at Jamie in horror. "Uh oh."

"This volcano isn't dormant at all," said Jamie. "It's active, and it's going to erupt!"

GRUMMBBLE!

The earth shook again, harder this time.

KABOOM!

The sound of a deafening explosion split the air and a massive cloud of black smoke blasted up from the volcano. Clouds of ash began billowing out of the volcano like a rolling wall of dust.

"Look out!" cried Tess. "It's heading straight for us!"

CHAPTER 5

"Run!" shouted Jamie.

The ash flow was very fast. Tess and Jamie turned and scrambled down between the steep banks of the streambed. Wanna sent up a cloud of spray as he charged ahead.

Tess looked back over her shoulder. "We've got to get out of this streambed!"

she yelled desperately. "The ash is using it like a channel. And it's traveling much faster than we are."

Jamie could see what she meant. The ash cloud was taking the quickest route to get down the volcano—and they were right in its path.

Spitting and crackling, the ash surged toward them. Jamie and Tess started to haul themselves up the slippery bank.

GRUNK! GRUNK!

Jamie looked back. Wanna was trying in vain to climb out after them!

"Quick, Wanna!" yelled Jamie.

"We have to help him," shouted Tess, above the roar of the cloud.

They flattened themselves on the bank, and Jamie could feel the heat of the approaching ash beginning to burn his arms. They each grabbed a paw and heaved Wanna to safety.

"Just in time!" said Tess, wiping the sweat from her forehead.

Wanna cowered behind them, watching the hot ash flow down the volcano. Rocks popped with heat as they were engulfed in the boiling mass.

They backed away, shielding their eyes from the glare.

"I've never felt anything so hot,"
said Jamie.

"We need to get to the plains," urged
Tess. "It's not safe here."

They skidded down the steep slope,
jumping over rocks and pushing through
ferns near the bottom, until they finally
ran out of breath.

Jamie took a quick glance behind them, and saw that the ash stream hadn't reached as far as the green lower slopes. "Hey," he panted. "I don't believe it. The ash cloud has stopped!"

Shielding her eyes, Tess followed Jamie's gaze. "It must have only been a little eruption," Tess guessed.

GRUNK!

Wanna bounded off again down the slope, looking back at them anxiously.

"I think he wants us to get off the mountain," said Jamie.

BOOM!

The friends ducked down, covering their ears, as another deafening explosion filled the air.

"Oh no!" cried Tess, pointing to the top of the volcano. "I think that was just the beginning!"

A huge plume of ash was shooting up into the sky from the crater, rapidly covering the bare rock.

"There's loads of the stuff!" Jamie shouted. "It's spilling out everywhere."

They didn't wait to see any more. Jamie and Tess hurtled down the slippery slope, with Wanna leading the way.

Rounding a dense clump of ferns Jamie and Tess suddenly found themselves surrounded by lizards and insects swarming around in panic. And the silly group of compsognathus were squawking around, feasting on the fleeing creatures.

"I don't believe it!" exclaimed Tess, trying not to crush anything underfoot.

"They don't seem to realize the volcano's spilling its guts up," Jamie said. "They just want snacks!"

Tess and Jamie looked at each other. "They're going to get fried," said Tess, with horror.

"We have to make them move," Jamie decided.

Tess waved her arms and ran at the compsognathus. They ignored him and continued snacking, chirping happily as they went.

"What are we going to do?" Jamie looked around for an answer. The ash had reached the top of the vegetation. Bushes and ferns disappeared, burned to ashes as they were engulfed by the rolling wall of dust.

"I've got an idea," shouted Tess.

Tess ran among the compsognathus, letting out a loud, "YAIEE!"

The little dinosaurs stopped and looked at her, their mouths gaping. Tess squawked again. "YAIEE!"

The compsos copied her.

YAIEE! YAIEE!

"Now that I have their attention, show them some food!" Tess yelled.

Jamie pulled another sandwich out of the backpack. He waved it at the compsognathus. They smelled the tuna and raced toward him, eyes shining greedily.

"Let's lure them away!" cried Tess.

Jamie held the sandwich above his head and the friends started to run down the mountain again. The band of greedy compsognathus scampered after them.

"We've got to go faster," yelled Tess. "It's getting closer."

They pounded along as fast as they could. Jamie wondered how long he could keep up the pace. His heart was

racing and his legs were hurting with
every step. And he knew that the
compsognathus couldn't run as long as
he could. The ash was gaining on them
with every second.

They were all going to be
swallowed up!

CHAPTER 6

With gasping breaths, Jamie and Tess crashed through the ferns. Wanna was in the lead and the compsognathus were running behind. Jamie could feel his heart almost bursting from his chest as he waited for the cloud to surge over him.

But nothing happened. At last, he couldn't bear it any longer. He threw a terrified glance over his shoulder.

He expected to see a wall of bubbling dust crash down on him like a huge wave. But there was nothing there. Wiping the sweat from his eyes, Jamie peered up the slope. High above, the ash was pouring into a new streambed. It had found a quicker way down the mountain.

Jamie bent over, trying to catch his breath. "We can stop!" he yelled to Tess. "The flow is heading away. Toward the Great Canyon."

"What a relief!" Tess punched the air.

"The canyon's deep enough to redirect it."

"That means Dino World is safe, and so are the compsognathus," added Jamie, as a bunch of the little dinos caught up with them. Soon the friends were surrounded by a sea of squawking dinosaurs, jumping for the sandwich that was still in Jamie's hand.

"Jump all you like!" Tess told them, laughing. "We're just glad you didn't get hurt."

Wanna ran around, crossly head-butting the excited compsognathus away, but they ignored him, and kept clamoring toward Jamie and Tess.

"This'll solve the problem" called Jamie.

He broke the sandwich into small pieces, holding it high above the compsognathus' heads. Then he threw the pieces in different directions.

All the compsognathus heads turned this way and that—and in an instant they scattered after the shower of food, squawking at the top of their voices. The fastest ones swept the pieces up in their teeth and the rest gave chase with their funny stiff-legged run.

"We've had an awesome adventure!" said Jamie, brushing volcanic dust out of his hair.

"Escape from the Jurassic Volcano," announced Tess. "It would make a great TV show. Although, come to think of it—it wasn't like any eruption I've ever seen in the movies. Maybe there are different types. We should ask your Mom!"

"Good idea, let's head home," said Jamie, turning toward Ginkgo Cave. "That reminds me, we should see how Mom's doing with her greedy dinosaurs."

They stopped at the edge of the jungle to take one last look at the Misty Mountains with the thick plume of smoke still rising from its crater.

Tess breathed a sigh of relief. "The flow's stopped now."

"There's a herd of brachiosaurs in the distance," said Jamie, pointing. "And some diplodocus nibbling at those trees over there."

"The dinosaurs are all coming back to the plains," said Tess. "They must know the danger's over."

"Everything's back to normal then," said Jamie.

"Well," said Tess, "normal for our Jurassic World. And that's…"

"AWESOME!" they shouted together.

"I can't wait to tell Dinosaur Club all about the volcano," said Jamie.

"And that not even boiling ash could stop the compsognathus from wanting their snacks!" added Tess with a grin.

They plunged toward the giant trees and splashed through a little river to get some of the volcanic dust off of them. Soon they had reached Ginkgo Cave.

Jamie picked three juicy ginkgoes from a nearby tree. "Those greedy compsos shouldn't have all the fun," he said as he tossed them to their little dinosaur friend.

Wanna stuffed them in his mouth all at once and settled down to chomp. Jamie and Tess waved goodbye, put their feet over the dino footprints, and walked backward into their own world.

As Jamie and Tess walked down the path to the beach, they heard shouts and cheers from below. A crowd of dinosaurs was waving and beckoning at them. Dr. Morgan was standing in the middle, looking frazzled.

"I don't think we'll be able to escape this bunch," said Jamie, as he and Tess headed along the beach.

"Thank goodness you're here!" Dr. Morgan called to them. "We're having a soccer match—carnivores versus herbivores. Will you two referee?"

She threw the ball to Jamie and the whistle to Tess. Jamie quickly put the ball down on the sand for kickoff and Tess blew the whistle to start the game.

In an instant every single soccer player was charging toward them! Tess and Jamie were soon buried under a pile of cheering dinosaurs. At last, a small pterodactyl got possession of the ball and all the others headed off after it, with a lot of prehistoric shrieking.

Jamie and Tess sat up and watched the eager herd head for the goal.

Tess grinned. "I wonder who'd win if they played the compsognathus!"

"I know one thing," answered Jamie. "I wouldn't want to be the referee for that match!"

Dinosaur time line

The Triassic
(250–200 million years ago)

The first period of the Mesozoic era was the Triassic. During the Triassic, there were very few plants, and the Earth was hot and dry, like a desert. Most of the dinosaurs that lived during the Triassic were small.

The Jurassic
(200–145 million years ago)

The second period of the Mesozoic era was the Jurassic. During the Jurassic, the Earth became cooler and wetter, which caused a lot of plants to grow. This created a lot of food for dinosaurs that helped them grow big and thrive.

The Cretaceous
(145–66 million years ago)

The third and final period of the Mesozoic era was the Cretaceous. During the Cretaceous, dinosaurs were at their peak and dominated the Earth, but at the end most of them suddenly became extinct.

Dinosaurs existed during a time on Earth known as the Mesozoic era. It lasted for more than 180 million years, and was split into three different periods: the Triassic, Jurassic, and the Cretaceous.

Notable dinosaurs from the Triassic

Plateosaurus

Coelophysis

Eoraptor

Notable dinosaurs from the Jurassic

Stegosaurus

Allosaurus

Archaeopteryx

Diplodocus

Notable dinosaurs from the Cretaceous

T. rex

Triceratops

Velociraptor

Iguanodon

DINO DATA

What this little predator lacked in size it made up for in speed. It was a swift hunter that ate lizards and small mammals, but it also scavenged meat from dead animals it found.

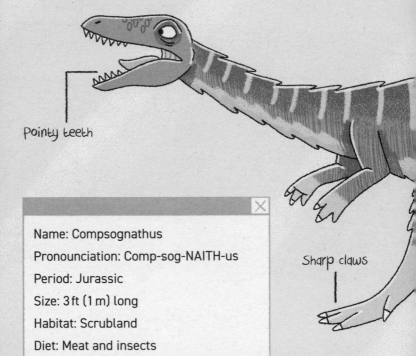

Pointy teeth

Sharp claws

Name: Compsognathus

Pronounciation: Comp-sog-NAITH-us

Period: Jurassic

Size: 3 ft (1 m) long

Habitat: Scrubland

Diet: Meat and insects

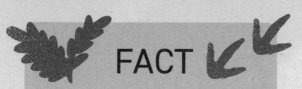

FACT

Compsognathus was about
the size of a turkey.

Skinny legs

FACT

Compsognathus had hollow
bones which helped it stay
light on its feet.

DINO DATA

Ankylosaurus was no helpless herbivore. Its thick armor and deadly tail helped it fend off the deadliest predators, including the mighty T. rex!

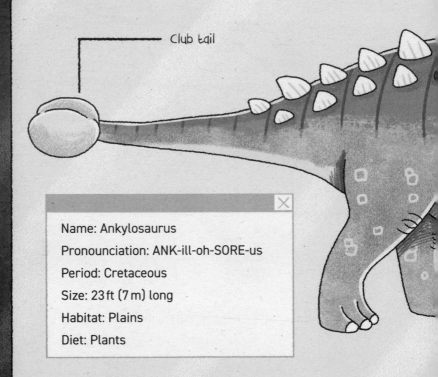

Club tail

Name: Ankylosaurus

Pronounciation: ANK-ill-oh-SORE-us

Period: Cretaceous

Size: 23 ft (7 m) long

Habitat: Plains

Diet: Plants

FACT

Ankylosaurus was covered in bony plates, making it like a dinosaur version of a tank

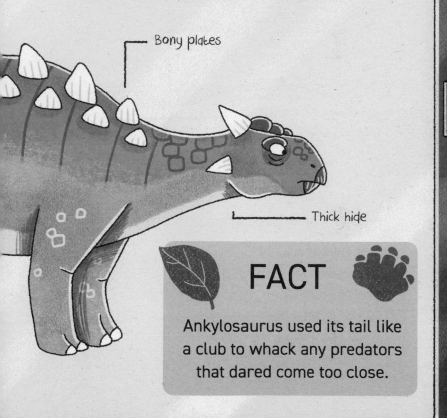

Bony plates

Thick hide

FACT

Ankylosaurus used its tail like a club to whack any predators that dared come too close.

DINO DATA

Wannanosaurus was a small dinosaur from the late Cretaceous period. It is known for having a very hard skull.

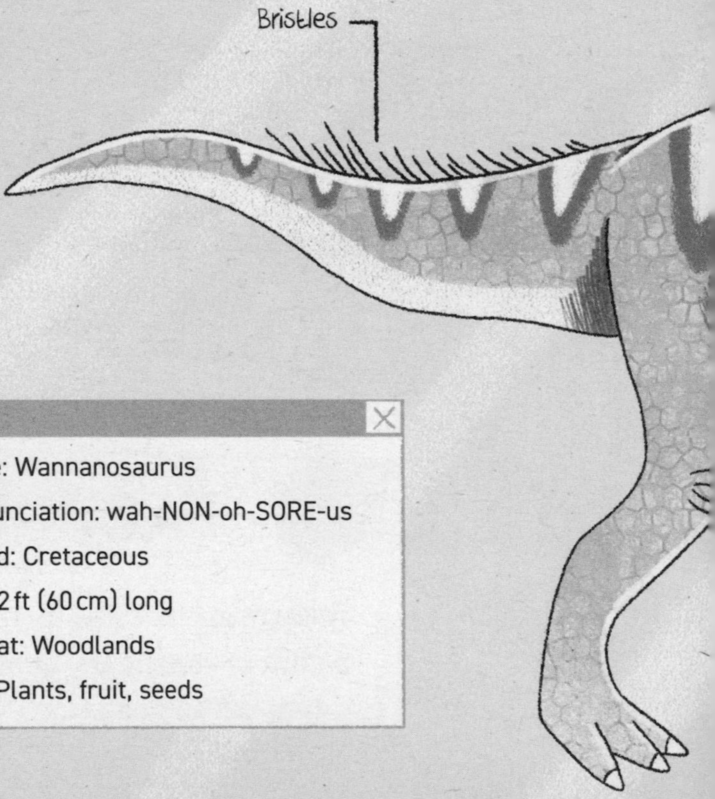

Bristles

Name: Wannanosaurus

Pronunciation: wah-NON-oh-SORE-us

Period: Cretaceous

Size: 2 ft (60 cm) long

Habitat: Woodlands

Diet: Plants, fruit, seeds

FACT

Wannanosaurus fossils were discovered in China.

Hard skull

FACT

Scientists aren't sure whether Wannanosaurus used its skull to defend itself from predators or to fight off rivals.

QUIZ

1   What does compsognathus mean?

2   True or false: The Misty Mountains are a dormant volcano.

3   What is the name of the land that existed before there were separate continents?

4   True or false: Wanna is an ankylosaurus.

5   What name does Tess give to herself, Jamie, and Wanna when they're exploring?

6   True or false: Some lizards have purple heads.

CHECK YOUR ANSWERS on page 95

GLOSSARY

AMMONITE
A type of sea creature that lived during the time of the dinosaurs

CARNIVORE
An animal that only eats meat

DINOSAUR
A group of ancient reptiles that lived millions of years ago

FOSSIL
Remains of a living thing that have become preserved over time

GINKGO
A type of tree that dates back millions of years

HERBIVORE
An animal that only eats plant matter

JURASSIC
The second period of the time dinosaurs existed (200-145 million years ago)

PALEONTOLOGIST
A scientist who studies dinosaurs and other fossils

PTEROSAUR
Ancient flying reptiles that existed at the same time as dinosaurs

PREDATOR
An animal that hunts other animals for food

QUIZ ANSWERS
1. Pretty jaw
2. False
3. Pangaea
4. False
5. The Jurassic trio
6. True

DK | Penguin Random House

Text for DK by Working Partners Ltd
9 Kingsway, London WC2B 6XF
With special thanks to Jan Burchett and Sara Vogler

For Sara O'Connor and everyone at Working Partners

Design by Collaborate Ltd
Illustrator Louise Forshaw
Consultant Dougal Dixon
Acquisitions Editor James Mitchem
Editor Becca Arlington
US Editor Jane Perlmutter
US Senior Editor Shannon Beatty
Senior Designer and Jacket Designer Elle Ward
Publishing Coordinator Issy Walsh
Production Editor Abi Maxwell
Production Controller Leanne Burke
Publishing Director Sarah Larter

First American Edition, 2022
Published in the United States by DK Publishing
1745 Broadway, 20th Floor, New York, NY 10019

A catalog record for this book is available from the Library of Congress.

ISBN: 978-0-7440-5985-4 (paperback)
ISBN: 978-0-7440-5986-1 (hardcover)

DK books are available at special discounts when purchased in bulk for sales
promotions, premiums, fund-raising, or educational use. For details, contact:
DK Publishing Special Markets, 1745 Broadway, 20th Floor, New York, NY 10019
SpecialSales@dk.com

Printed and bound in Great Britain by
Clays Ltd, Elcograf S.p.A.

www.dk.com
For the curious